D0461397

PROLOGUE

In a museum there hangs a painting by Henri Rousseau titled
The Sleeping Gypsy.

People looking at it wonder: Who is the girl in the painting? Why is
she sleeping under the full moon in the desert? Is that a guitar next to her?
Will she play it? Will the lion standing over her just sniff at her and wander off?
Or will he eat her up? This book suggests some answers to these questions.

For Theron Raines
1925–2012
one of the last true gentlemen

and for my editor, Grace Maccarone,
without whom this book would not have happened

THE SLEEPING GYPSY

MORDICAI GERSTEIN

HOLIDAY HOUSE ✶ NEW YORK

One night, Henri Rousseau dreamed of a girl walking alone across a desert.

All day the girl and the sun had traveled in opposite directions. Now, behind her, the sun silently descended.

Before her, under a dome of darkening sky, she saw endless hills of soft sand tinted pink by the twilight.

The girl came to a river. She filled her clay bottle
with water and sat on the warm, soft sand.

From her cloth bundle she
took bread, sweet dates
and tart, salty cheese.
She ate and drank.
One by one,
stars
appeared.

The girl picked up her mandolin, and as her fingers plucked and pressed the strings, she sang.

Her voice seemed to bring the stars closer,
as if they were leaning down to hear.

When her song ended, she heard
its echoes singing to other
echoes, which sang to
others, farther and
farther, till she
could hear
no
more.

She lay down on the soft, warm sand, shut her eyes
and fell asleep.

Slowly, shyly the moon rose like a lonely
eye, curious, watching.

Near her feet a lizard squatted,
staring at her toes.

A rabbit hopped and waited . . .
hopped and waited, till she was
close to the girl's face.

A snake slithered up.
"I've never heard a song like that,"
she said. "Where did this girl
come from?"

"Where is she going?" asked an ostrich who joined them.

"Why is she here?" asked the lizard.

"What's her name?" asked a young mother baboon.

"Is she a lost tourist?" asked the moon.

"Maybe she is a musician
looking for an audience,"
suggested the rabbit.

"Has she run away from home?"
asked the snake.

"Is she a princess looking
for her prince?" said an old
tortoise dragging itself close.

"She is MINE!" roared
a lion who leaped from
behind a dune.

He stood over the girl, his mane full
of moonlight, and sniffed at her hair.

The ostrich then noticed a figure
silhouetted against the sky.
"Now, who can this be?" she said.
The others turned and saw it too.

"It's the prince!"
said the lizard.

"Is it the tour
guide?" said
the baboon.

"Is it her audience?" said the moon.

"I hope it's a lion hunter," said the lion, "come to be EATEN UP!"

It was a man carrying a wooden case. He wore an artist's beret. "Good evening," he said, bowing slightly. "I am Henri Rousseau. We are all in a dream. It is *my* dream. The girl is here, as are all of you, so that I may paint a picture."

He opened his case, unfolded an
easel and put a canvas on it.

He squeezed bright worms
of paint onto a palette.

"You, Lion, stay just where you are and lift your tail a bit. Baboon, stay to the left. Rabbit, move to the right, next to the tortoise. Ostrich and Snake, raise your heads, please."

"And what shall *I* do?" asked the moon.

"Just smile and continue to do what you are doing," said
the artist. The man studied the arrangement and began
to paint.

After a while, the baboon, not able to contain her curiosity, scampered around behind Rousseau to see how the picture was progressing.

"You've made my nose too big," she said.
"Hmmm," said Rousseau, and scraped her out of the picture.

The snake then had to slither over and see for herself.
"You made me too fat," she said.

Rousseau erased her too.

The rabbit and tortoise joined the others.

"The girl is too ugly," said the tortoise.
"My ears are too short," said the rabbit.
"Make the guitar bigger," said the ostrich.
"I think it should be smaller," said the lizard.
Rousseau ignored their comments, as he did all criticism.
He simply scraped them all out of the picture.
Only the lion stood still and proud in the moon's light.

"Paint my mane beautifully," he said,
"or you will be my BREAKFAST!"

The hours passed. Henri Rousseau stepped back from
his painting, tilted his head to the right and squinted.

"I'll finish the painting in the morning," he said.

He wiped his brushes and repacked the easel. "Good night,
and thank you all," he said, bowing to the assembled
creatures.

The animals watched him disappear among dunes.
Then they too wandered off, each in his or her own
way, each toward home.

All except the lion. He stood watch over the girl until
the first flare of sun appeared at the edge of the desert,
and then . . .

. . . in Paris, Henri Rousseau awoke and the girl, the lion and the desert all faded away. Rousseau stretched, got out of bed and put the finishing touches on his picture.

AUTHOR'S NOTE

I first saw a reproduction of Henri Rousseau's painting *The Sleeping Gypsy* (1897) in a magazine when I was eight or nine and was fascinated by its sense of danger and mystery.

Born in 1844, the French painter Henri Rousseau worked in Paris as a civil servant and didn't begin to paint seriously until he was in his midforties. He had no formal art training and was quoted as saying, "I've had no teacher other than nature." He became famous for his fantastical jungle scenes, painted from his imagination. He had never been to a jungle or desert, and the only wild animals he ever saw were in the zoo. When he first exhibited his pictures, the public and most critics thought they were childlike and naive. But many young artists of the day, such as Picasso and Matisse—those who would invent "modern art"—appreciated his work and were influenced by it.

Rousseau died in 1910. *The Sleeping Gypsy*, one of his best-known paintings, has a subtitle which reads, "Although the Predatory animal is wild, it hesitates to leap upon its victim, who has fallen asleep from exhaustion." *The Sleeping Gypsy* is in the collection of the Museum of Modern Art in New York City, where you may see it.

Copyright © 2016 by Mordicai Gerstein

All Rights Reserved

HOLIDAY HOUSE is registered in the U.S. Patent and Trademark Office.

Printed and Bound in April 2016 at Toppan Leefung, DongGuan City, China.

The artwork was created with acrylic paint on Fabriano watercolor paper and digital tools.

www.holidayhouse.com

First Edition

1 3 5 7 9 10 8 6 4 2

Library of Congress Cataloging-in-Publication Data

Names: Gerstein, Mordicai, author, illustrator.

Title: The sleeping gypsy / Mordicai Gerstein.

Description: First edition. | New York : Holiday House, [2016] | Summary: "An imagined story about Henri Rousseau's famous painting tells why a lion and a gypsy are in the painting and a lizard, a rabbit, a turtle, and other animals are not"— Provided by publisher.

Identifiers: LCCN 2015045405 | ISBN 9780823421428 (hardcover)

Subjects: | CYAC: Rousseau, Henri, 1844-1910—Fiction. | Art—Fiction. | Artists—Fiction. | Dreams—Fiction. | Animals—Fiction.

Classification: LCC PZ7.G325 Sk 2016 | DDC [E]—dc23

LC record available at http://lccn.loc.gov/2015045405